Belle's Library

A COLLECTION OF LITERARY QUOTATIONS
AND INSPIRATIONAL MUSINGS

Printed in the United States of America
First Hardcover Edition, January 2017
3 5 7 9 10 8 6 4
FAC-008598-17048
Library of Congress Control Number: 2016952971
ISBN 978-1-4847-8099-2

Designed by Jenna Huerta and Gegham Vardanyan

Visit disneybooks.com and disney.com/beautyandthebeast

SUSTAINABLE Certified Sourcing
FORESTRY
INITIATIVE www.sfiprogram.org
SFI-00993
Logo Applies to Text Stock Only

Belle's *Library*

A COLLECTION OF LITERARY QUOTATIONS AND INSPIRATIONAL MUSINGS

Foreword by LINDA WOOLVERTON
Written by BRITTANY RUBIANO
Art by JENNA HUERTA

Screenplay by EVAN SPILIOTOPOULOS
and STEPHEN CHBOSKY and BILL CONDON

DISNEP PRESS

Los Angeles • New York

Contents

Foreword by
Linda Woolverton

I grew up in a household where intellect and education were valued above all things. My father would not even allow a television to come through the front door. Rather, he joined the Heritage Club. Once a month, an impeccably bound and illustrated Door to Adventure and Faraway Places would arrive on our front step. I would lose myself in Rudyard Kipling, Madeleine L'Engle, William Shakespeare, Jane Austen, Joseph Conrad, Robert Louis Stevenson, L. Frank

Baum, Ernest Hemingway, Jack London, Victor Hugo, Lewis Carroll, and on and on. I inhaled literature.

These great authors invited me to dream. I dreamed of having tea with a Buddhist monk in the mountains of Tibet; of swimming with dolphins off an island in Greece; of sailing around Cape Horn in a tall ship; of living in Pompeii in the shadow of Mount Vesuvius. Of course, I was always the hero of my own dreams.

My favorite real-world place was the local public library, which was situated on the shoreline of Alamitos Bay in Long Beach, California. I often sat on the floor in the children's section with the light streaming in through the tall windows and the white sails of the small boats gliding past in the quiet bay beyond. It was a warm, safe place from which I could launch myself into exquisitely dangerous, heart-stopping adventures. That small sun-filled library on the bay was one of the greatest gifts of my childhood.

At home, however, my mother would sometimes rudely interrupt my reading with a chore. She often asked me to walk to the local market to pick up something that she'd forgotten for dinner. I remember being annoyed because she would invariably make this request just as I was coming to the most crucial part of the story. I would sigh and put my book down to run the errand. But one day, I absolutely could not put the book down, so I kept reading as I walked to the store. I stumbled a few times that first day. But I knew the way well, and soon, I mastered the skill. I would walk to the store, walk through it, grab the butter or bread, even pay, with barely a glance up. After a while, the storekeepers would see me coming and open the door for me.

Years later, I had the privilege of conjuring up a Disney heroine for an animated, musical retelling of the French fairy tale "Beauty and the Beast." My collaborator, the lyricist Howard Ashman, and I were very excited about creating a Disney heroine who led with her brains, not her looks. And we were even more excited about the possibility of making her a reader.

When Howard and I advanced this idea that Belle was a "bookworm," there were concerns from our colleagues that reading was too sedentary an occupation for film. It would be boring to watch Belle just sit around and read. My thoughts traveled back to that little market of my childhood. That was an easy problem to solve.

I suggested that Belle read as she walked through the village. She knows the way so well, she never even has to look up. This became the inspiration for the opening sequence of the film and the song "Belle."

I am so delighted to read the names of all the authors in Belle's fantasy-come-true library at the castle. I invite you to find a warm, safe place, or even a familiar path that you know very well, and launch yourself through these Doors to Adventure and Faraway Places.

READ AND DREAM.
Linda Woolverton

A noted screenwriter, author, and playwright, Linda Woolverton has penned numerous modern classics, including Beauty and the Beast (1991), The Lion King (1994), Alice in Wonderland (2010), and Maleficent (2014).

Belle's Book List

Aesop's Fables
by Aesop

— • —

Antony and Cleopatra
by William Shakespeare

— • —

The Blazing World
by Margaret Cavendish

— • —

The Book of the Thousand Nights and a Night
by Anonymous

— • —

The Canterbury Tales
by Geoffrey Chaucer

— • —

Don Quixote
by Miguel de Cervantes

— • —

The Fairy Tales of Charles Perrault
by Charles Perrault

— • —

Gulliver's Travels
by Jonathan Swift

A Midsummer Night's Dream
by William Shakespeare

– • –

The Misanthrope
by Molière

– • –

Le Morte d'Arthur
by Sir Thomas Malory

– • –

The *Odyssey*
by Homer

– • –

Oroonoko
by Aphra Behn

– • –

The Princess of Clèves
by Madame de La Fayette

– • –

Romeo and Juliet
by William Shakespeare

– • –

The Rover
by Aphra Behn

Belle's Literary
Journal

"

What's in a name? that which we call a rose
By any other name would smell as sweet.

"

– William Shakespeare, *Romeo and Juliet* –

No truer words have been spoken.

Whatever the name, the label applied—odd,

funny, <u>beast</u>—it does not matter.

It is one's essence,

what's on the inside,

that counts.

"

For, O my Friends! (said he) it is not Titles make Men brave, or good; or Birth that bestows Courage and Generosity, or makes the Owner happy.

"

– Aphra Behn, *Oroonoko* –

I believe Madame Behn's astute observation also relates to what I have experienced. One can be born with the best name or title, with the highest amount of power and privilege, but it is neither label nor station that determines one's character. And that is what really matters.

"

Money and jewels still, we find,
Stamp strong impressions on the mind.
But sweet discourse more potent riches yields;
Of higher value is the pow'r it wields.

"

– Charles Perrault, *The Fairy Tales of Charles Perrault*, "The Fairy" –

There are more important things
in this world than wealth.
As Monsieur Perrault's
fairy tale proclaims,
compassion is worth
a great deal—as are
courage and wit and generosity!
It is too bad those traits are not
the currency of choice. Or . . . maybe
they are, when it counts.

"

He may perhaps increase her bags, but not her family.

"

– Aphra Behn, *The Rover* –

Exactement.

All too often, people choose to associate
themselves with those who have riches,
looking no further than their coin purses.
I love the people in my life
who better my heart
and mind,
like Papa.

"

Let's be men; on all occasions
Show in our words the truth that's in our hearts,
Letting the heart itself speak out, not hiding
Our feelings under masks of compliment.

"

– Molière, *The Misanthrope* –

I am a firm believer
in speaking your mind.
It does no good to mask your
frankest thoughts,
your truest feelings.

(The exception being, of course, when those thoughts
or feelings will serve only to hurt others.
I feel this is an important distinction in
Monsieur Molière's delightful play, too.)

"

The hero is brave in deeds as well as words.

"

– Aesop, *Aesop's Fables*, "The Hunter and the Woodman" –

On the other side of the coin,
it seems equally important
to follow declarations
with <u>actions</u>
that support them.
Or more simply put—say what
you mean, do as you say.

"

Stranger, in truth thou speakest these things with kindly thought, as a father to his son, and never will I forget them.

"

– Homer, the *Odyssey* –

Oh, how I love this scene—Athena
traveling down to Earth to help the poor
mortals, paying a visit to Odysseus's son,
Telemachus, in disguise; Telemachus
responding to his strange guest
with benevolence and gratitude.
It is an exchange that affects him
forever, and one that reminds me
of another extraordinary visit.

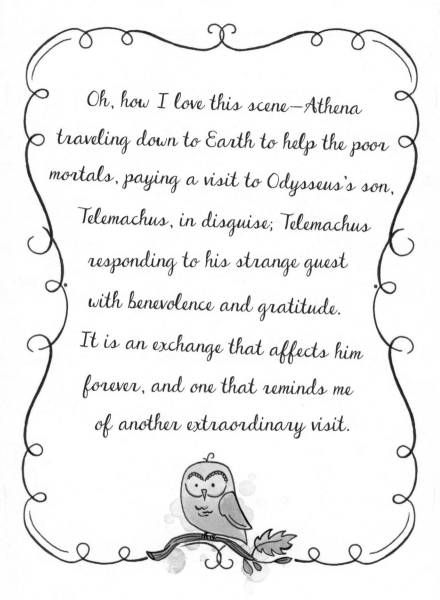

66

'You are so very pretty, my dear, so good and so mannerly, that I cannot help giving you a gift' (for this was a Fairy, who had taken the form of a poor country-woman, to see how far the civility and good manners of this pretty girl would go). 'I will give you a gift,' continued the Fairy.

99

– Charles Perrault, *The Fairy Tales of Charles Perrault*, "The Fairy" –

Indeed, showing kindness to strangers goes a long way. Really, you should always treat others the way you would wish to be treated. You never know what their unique circumstances might be.

"

Monsieur de Nemours locked himself up in his own room, being unable to contain his joy at having in his possession a portrait of Madame de Clèves. He felt all the happiness that love can give.

"

– Madame de La Fayette, *The Princess of Clèves* –

I think Papa would like this passage.
A portrait of a loved one can evoke
so many emotions, reminding one of things
that have been, or inspiring
dreams of what may come.
What power
the paintbrush
has!

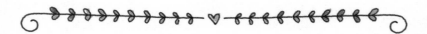

"

For nature had with sov'reign diligence
Y-formed her in so great excellence,
As though she wouldë say, 'Lo, I, Natúre,
Thus can I form and paint a creature,
When that me list; who can me counterfeit?'

"

– Geoffrey Chaucer, *The Canterbury Tales*, "The Physician's Tale" –

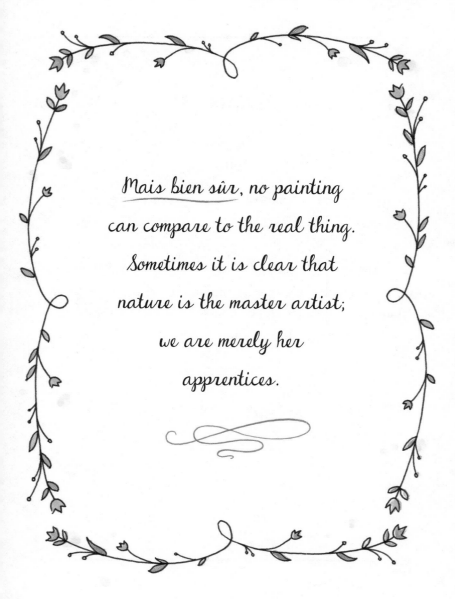

Mais bien sûr, no painting
can compare to the real thing.
Sometimes it is clear that
nature is the master artist;
we are merely her
apprentices.

"

There was once in times of yore and ages long gone before,
a great and puissant King . . . who . . . surpassed each and
every in wit and wisdom. He was generous, open handed
and beneficent, and he gave to those who sought him and
repelled not those who resorted to him; and he comforted
the broken-hearted and honourably entreated those who
fled to him for refuge.

"

– Anonymous, *The Book of the Thousand Nights and a Night,*
"The Ebony Horse" –

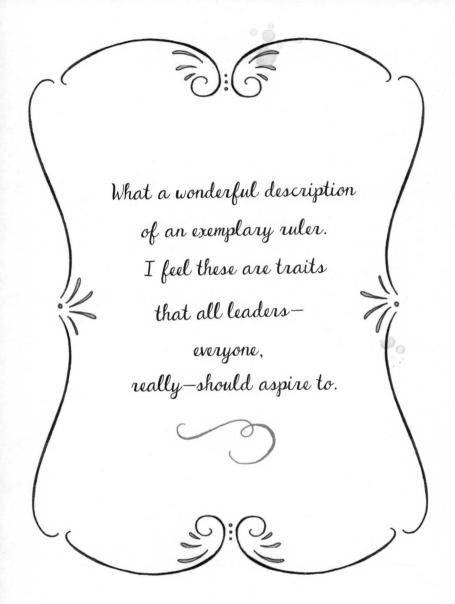

What a wonderful description
of an exemplary ruler.
I feel these are traits
that all leaders—
everyone,
really—should aspire to.

66

But great allowances should be given to a king, who lives wholly secluded from the rest of the world, and must therefore be altogether unacquainted with the manners and customs that most prevail in other nations: the want of which knowledge will ever produce many prejudices, and a certain narrowness of thinking.

99

– Jonathan Swift, *Gulliver's Travels* –

And here is a king who is not so ideal.
Learning about other cultures and
customs is especially important
for one in power. Such knowledge
can create a certain openness,
a society of mutual betterment,
and a celebratory fraternité
across different lands,
which will only
strengthen us all.

"

We should scrutinise ourselves no little
Before assuming to condemn our neighbours,
And add the weight of exemplary living
To any censure that we pass on others.

"

– Molière, *The Misanthrope* –

It can be so easy to judge others—
sometimes for their differences,
sometimes for undesired similarities.
But it does no good to critique,
especially if, as Monsieur Molière
suggests, you do not study your _own_
reflection first. Which, of course,
can be quite difficult,
even at the best of times.

"

If you are divided among yourselves,
you will be broken as easily as these sticks.

"

– Aesop, *Aesop's Fables*, "The Father and His Sons" –

I wish the villagers would read
this story. If we are united, we will
surely thrive, just as a bundle
of sticks is stronger than the
sticks individually.
When there is division among us,
there is a greater chance
that we will fall.

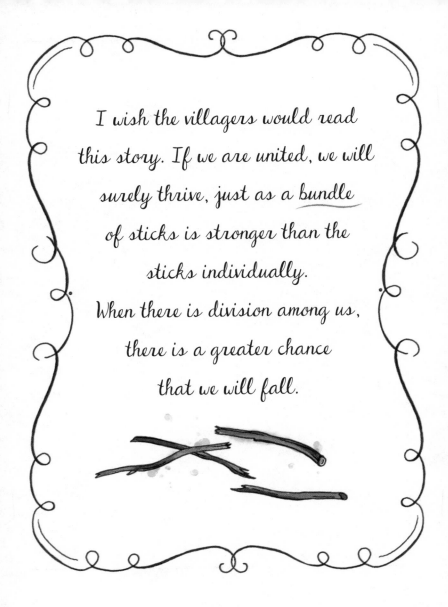

"

I had rather die in the adventure of noble achievements,
than live in obscure and sluggish security.

"

– Margaret Cavendish, *The Blazing World* –

I think about this quotation often.
I have always wanted to leave
the village and seek adventure.
I long to be remembered for _something_,
even if that something
is merely the pursuit
of my dreams.

"

Everyone is the son of his works.

"

– Miguel de Cervantes, *Don Quixote* –

An inspiring message, to be sure!
That your identity is linked to your
works, to your
accomplishments,
not to your lineage or the
preconceptions of your society.
That people of all walks of life, from
all parts of the world, can do anything
and be remembered for what
they have done.

"

He diverted himself with viewing the various cities and
countries over which he passed and which he knew not,
never having seen them in his life. Amongst the rest, he
descried a city ordered after the fairest fashion in the midst
of a verdant and riant land, rich in trees and streams,
with gazelles pacing daintily over the plains; whereat he fell
a-musing and said to himself, 'Would I knew the name of
yon town and in what land it is!'

"

– Anonymous, *The Book of the Thousand Nights and a Night*,
"The Ebony Horse" –

This is such a wonderful passage!
The prince flying on his magical
wooden horse, taking in the wonders
of the foreign lands before him.
I cannot wait to experience the joys of travel!

"

And it must be confessed, that from the great intercourse of trade and commerce between both realms . . . there are few persons of distinction, or merchants, or seamen, who dwell in the maritime parts, but what can hold conversation in both tongues.

"

– Jonathan Swift, *Gulliver's Travels* –

Monsieur Swift provides another exciting aspect of voyaging (or living in a trading city): the opportunity to learn other languages.
What insight and pleasure one must gain in parlaying with someone from another country. And learning the nuances of different words, of entirely new phrases—
quel magnifique!

"

I was born free, and that I might live in freedom I chose the solitude of the fields; in the trees of the mountains I find society, the clear waters of the brooks are my mirrors, and to the trees and waters I make known my thoughts and charms. I am a fire afar off, a sword laid aside.

"

– Miguel de Cervantes, *Don Quixote* –

What a stunning description.
The natural world is so full of
splendor and wonder.
I know I enjoy wandering
the nearby fields whenever
I need to take my leave of society
(mostly Gaston).

"

This horse ceased not running till he stood before the whelp, the son of the lion who, when he saw him, marvelled and made much of him and said, 'What is thy kind, O majestic wild beast, and wherefore fleest thou into this desert wide and vast?' He replied, 'O lord of wild beasts, I am a steed of the horse-kind, and the cause of my running is that I am fleeing from the son of Adam.'

"

– Anonymous, *The Book of the Thousand Nights and a Night*,
"The Birds and Beasts and the Carpenter" –

The majestic horse from this tale reminds me of Philippe—so smart and swift. Philippe is like family to Papa and me.

It is so awful that there are those who mistreat the fine animals that live in this world.

"

'Alas!' said the Horse, 'if you really wish me to be in good condition, you should groom me less, and feed me more.'

"

– Aesop, *Aesop's Fables*, "The Horse and Groom" –

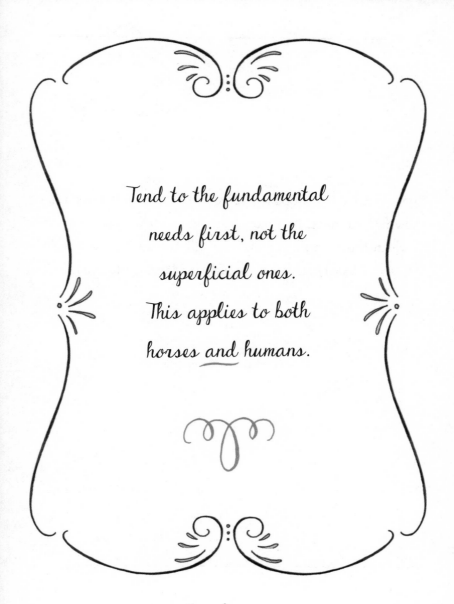

Tend to the fundamental
needs first, not the
superficial ones.
This applies to both
horses and humans.

"

When a lady is proposed to you for a wife, you never ask
how fair, discreet, or virtuous she is; but what's her fortune;
which if but small, you cry 'she will not do my business,'
and basely leave her, though she languish for you.
Say, is not this as poor?

"

– Aphra Behn, *The Rover* –

It is my firm belief that a woman
is worth _much more_ than her dowry.
Moreover, she is not simply a decorative
ornament or bearer of children,
despite what Gaston might think.

"

And certes, Sir, though none authority
Were in no book, ye gentles of honoúr
Say, that men should an oldë wight honoúr,
And call him father, for your gentleness;
And authors shall I finden, as I guess.
Now there ye say that I am foul and old,
Then dread ye not to be a cokëwold.

"

– Geoffrey Chaucer, *The Canterbury Tales*, "The Wife of Bath's Tale" –

Another unfair conception—
that when a woman ages,
she grows less and less
appealing, but when
a man ages, he becomes
an honored gentleman.
Surely this is an
assumption we can change.

"

All this was done in a moment. Fairies are
not long in doing their business.

"

– Charles Perrault, *The Fairy Tales of Charles Perrault*,
"The Sleeping Beauty in the Wood" –

It seems to me that
this is actually
quite accurate.

"

'Thou mayest well believe that,' answered Don Quixote,
'because, either I know little, or this castle is enchanted.'

"

– Miguel de Cervantes, *Don Quixote* –

I can say with the utmost
authority, there are certain signs
that a castle is enchanted.

You will know them
when you see them.

"

My taste is for freedom, and I have no relish for constraint.

"

– Miguel de Cervantes, *Don Quixote* –

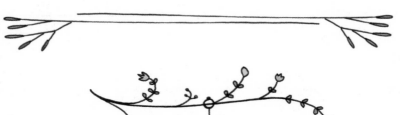

I don't believe anyone
can really be happy
if they are not free.

"

Our prison, for it may none other be.
Fortune hath giv'n us this adversity.

"

– Geoffrey Chaucer, *The Canterbury Tales*, "The Knight's Tale" –

There are many different types
of prisons—true stone fortresses,
stockades of society, pens of the
mind, shackles of the soul.
But they all have the same effect—
to dim the light inside
a little bit at a time until it is
completely extinguished.
Freedom is like water, air,
sunlight. It is vital.

"

But come now, tarry, eager though thou art to be gone,
in order that when thou hast bathed and satisfied thy heart
to the full, thou mayest go to thy ship glad in spirit,
and bearing a gift costly and very beautiful, which shall be
to thee an heirloom from me, even such a gift
as dear friends give to friends.

"

– Homer, the *Odyssey* –

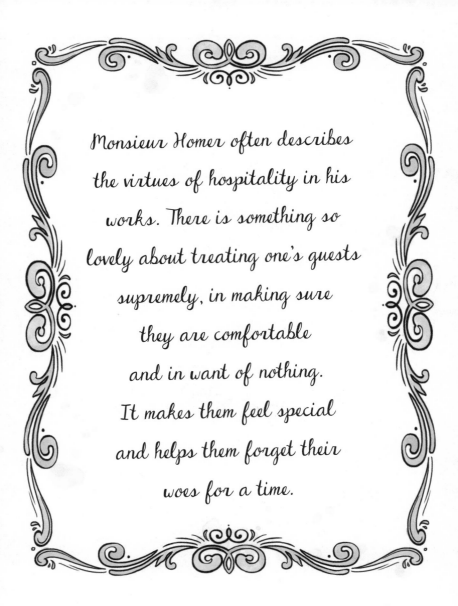

Monsieur Homer often describes
the virtues of hospitality in his
works. There is something so
lovely about treating one's guests
supremely, in making sure
they are comfortable
and in want of nothing.
It makes them feel special
and helps them forget their
woes for a time.

The fruit of every tale is for to say;
They eat and drink, and dance, and sing, and play.

– Geoffrey Chaucer, *The Canterbury Tales*, "The Man of Law's Tale" –

Lumiere,

par exemple,

is one of the best
hosts I know.
I think he would
enjoy this quotation
as much as I do.

"

If you were foolish enough to sing all the summer,
you must dance supperless to bed in the winter.

"

– Aesop, *Aesop's Fables*, "The Ants and the Grasshopper" –

An important lesson,
to be sure. It never hurts to
work hard and prepare
(as best you can)
for difficult times ahead.

"

Ah! so it is that miserable man,
By nature fickle, blind, unwise, and rash,
Oft fails to reap a harvest from great gifts
Bestowed upon him by the heav'nly gods.

"

– Charles Perrault, *The Fairy Tales of Charles Perrault*,
"The Ridiculous Wishes" –

One must, of course, first _see_
the goods and tools at one's
disposal in order to take
advantage of them. It does no
good to lament what one does
not have before looking at
what one does.

66

'Never more pray to me for help, until you have done
your best to help yourself, or depend upon it
you will henceforth pray in vain.'
Self-help is the best help.

99

– Aesop, *Aesop's Fables*, "Hercules and the Wagoner" –

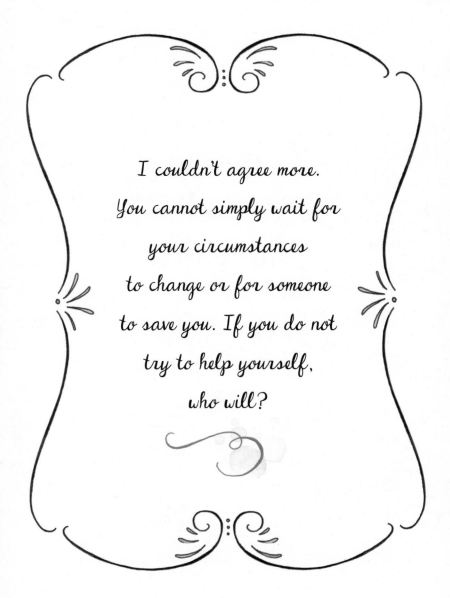

I couldn't agree more.
You cannot simply wait for
your circumstances
to change or for someone
to save you. If you do not
try to help yourself,
who will?

"

Yet some men say in many parts of England that King Arthur is not dead, but . . . that he shall come again. . . . I will not say it shall be so, but rather I will say, here in this world he changed his life.

"

– Sir Thomas Malory, *Le Morte d'Arthur* –

It is difficult to say what
one's legacy will be.
What will we leave behind
after we are gone?
All we can do is navigate through
the world we live in—however strange
or unfair it can sometimes be—and
rise to the occasions presented to us,
just as King Arthur did.
Mothers are taken too soon,
curses are cast, but _we_ control how
we react and how we are remembered.

"

The Pictures of the Pen shall out-last those of the Pencil,
and even Worlds themselves.

"

– Aphra Behn, *Oroonoko* –

I adore this quotation.
Books, poems, letters—there is
a certain power and
longevity in the written word.
I love to imagine people
decades or even centuries from now
enjoying the same works I do.

"

Said the Empress, you were recommended to me by an honest and ingenious spirit. Surely, answered the Duchess, the spirit is ignorant of my handwriting.

"

– Margaret Cavendish, *The Blazing World* –

I can relate to the poor duchess.
Sometimes it's difficult
to control the pen
when one is inspired.

"

Sound judgment always will avoid extremes,
And will be sober even in its virtue.

"

– Molière, *The Misanthrope* –

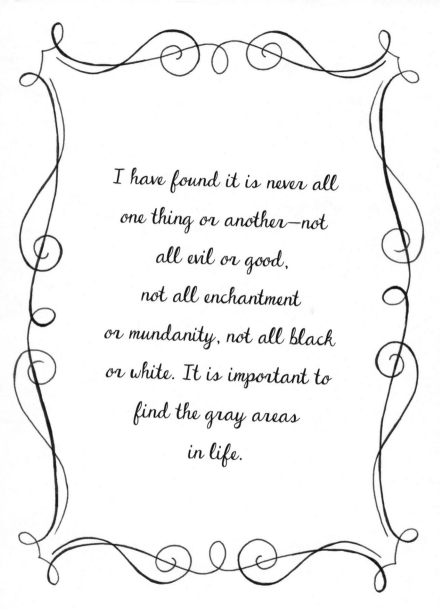

I have found it is never all
one thing or another—not
all evil or good,
not all enchantment
or mundanity, not all black
or white. It is important to
find the gray areas
in life.

"

I perceive that the greatest happiness in all the worlds consist in moderation.

"

– Margaret Cavendish, *The Blazing World* –

Though it is difficult
to achieve, balance
in all things is most admirable,
n'est-ce pas?

"

I was beadle of a brotherhood, and the beadle's gown
sat so well on me that all said I looked as if I was to be
steward of the same brotherhood. What will it be, then,
when I put a duke's robe on my back, or dress myself in
gold and pearls like a foreign count? I believe they'll come a
hundred leagues to see me.

"

– Miguel de Cervantes, *Don Quixote* –

Sancho's observation is quite interesting. If dressed perfectly for a specific role, can one assume that identity seamlessly? Is life merely a performance where those donning the best accoutrements get the best parts? If so, then I would prefer to play a practical role, one with sensible shoes and pockets to store books.

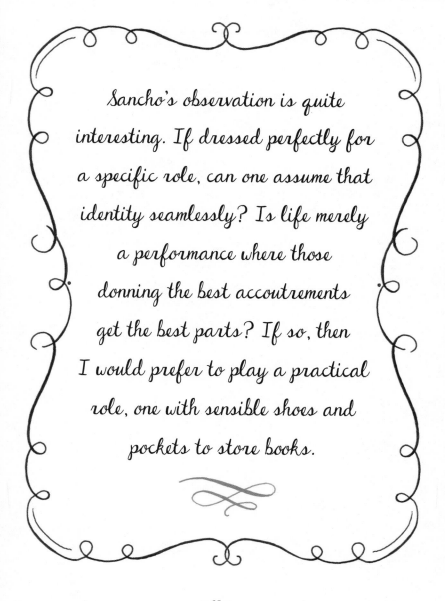

"

It must be remark'd of fine clothes how they move.

"

– Charles Perrault, *The Fairy Tales of Charles Perrault*, "The Master Cat" –

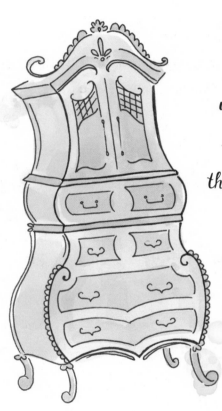

Madame
de Garderobe
would love these
remarks about
the effects of fine
clothing.

"

'If you judge from appearances here,' replied Madame de Chartres, 'you will be often mistaken; what appears is seldom the truth.'

"

– Madame de La Fayette, *The Princess of Clèves* –

I love Madame de La Fayette's
words of wisdom.
There is often
much more
to any given situation
than meets the eye.

66

Fine feathers don't make fine birds.

99

– Aesop, *Aesop's Fables*, "The Peacock and the Crane" –

C'est vrai. Appearances
can be deceiving.
Just because one's
plumage is attractive
does not mean one's
temperament matches.

"

Over hill, over dale,
Thorough bush, thorough brier,
Over park, over pale,
Thorough flood, thorough fire:
I do wander everywhere
Swifter than the moonës sphere,
And I serve the Fairy Queen
To dew her orbs upon the green.

"

– William Shakespeare, *A Midsummer Night's Dream* –

Monsieur Shakespeare
simply delights my imagination
with this section.

"

In oldë dayës of the king Arthoúr,
Of which that Britons speakë great honoúr,
All was this land full fill'd of faërie;
The Elf-queen, with her jolly company,
Danced full oft in many a green mead.
This was the old opinion, as I read;
I speak of many hundred years ago.

"

– Geoffrey Chaucer, *The Canterbury Tales*, "The Wife of Bath's Tale" –

Oh, how I long to visit the fairies
in Shakespeare's midsummer, or in
Chaucer's England of old.
There is a certain nostalgia
embedded in these lines for a time
that may never have existed.
Well, that is not quite right.
It exists in the pages of these works,
in the special little nooks and
crannies of the mind.

"

[Shahrázád] had perused the books, annals and legends of
preceding Kings, and the stories, examples and instances
of by-gone men and things; indeed it was said that she had
collected a thousand books of histories relating to antique
races and departed rulers. She had perused the works
of the poets and knew them by heart; she had studied
philosophy and the sciences, arts and accomplishments;
and she was pleasant and polite, wise and witty, well read
and well bred.

"

– Anonymous, *The Book of the Thousand Nights and a Night*,
"Story of King Shahryar and His Brother" –

Shahrázád is a character
after my own heart—reading and studying
as much as she can, using her wits
to escape her plight. She is one of my
favorite parts of the thousand
and one nights,

absolument!

"

And eke she leftë not, for no hunting,
To have of sundry tonguës full knowing,
When that she leisure had, and for t'intend
To learnë bookës was all her liking,
How she in virtue might her life dispend.

"

– Geoffrey Chaucer, *The Canterbury Tales*, "The Monk's Tale" –

Ah, Zenobia—another
woman of note.
Her love of language
and literature
is most admirable.

"

Having listened more attentively, she heard one say:
'Bring me that pot'; another 'Give me that kettle'; and a
third, 'Put some wood upon the fire.'. . . [They] began to
work, keeping time, to the tune of a very harmonious song.

"

– Charles Perrault, *The Fairy Tales of Charles Perrault*,
"Riquet with the Tuft" –

As Mrs. Potts has often said,
most troubles seem less troubling
after a bracing cup of tea.
Indeed, such a simple thing can
do wonders for the soul.
I love this image of the motions
of tea making as a sort of
dance—full of grace
and harmony.

66

Civil behaviour costs indeed some pains,
Requires of complaisance some little share;
But soon or late its due reward it gains,
And meets it often when we're not aware.

99

– Charles Perrault, *The Fairy Tales of Charles Perrault*, "The Fairy" –

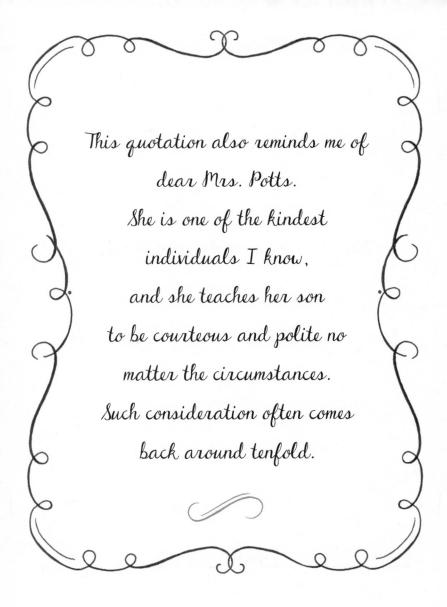

This quotation also reminds me of
dear Mrs. Potts.
She is one of the kindest
individuals I know,
and she teaches her son
to be courteous and polite no
matter the circumstances.
Such consideration often comes
back around tenfold.

"

As nearly as I may
I'll play the penitent to you, but mine honesty
Shall not make poor my greatness; nor my power
Work without it.

"

– William Shakespeare, *Antony and Cleopatra* –

It can be quite difficult not to let pride
or vanity stand in the way of
making an apology.
But admitting one's mistakes
does not diminish
any power or greatness.
In fact, such honesty is honorable.
It is a sign of a worthy leader.

"

Thou Sir Launcelot, there thou liest, that thou were never matched of earthly knight's hand. And thou were the courteoust knight that ever bare shield. And thou were the truest friend to thy lover that ever bestrad horse. And thou were the truest lover of a sinful man that ever loved woman. And thou were the kindest man that ever struck with sword.

"

– Sir Thomas Malory, *Le Morte d'Arthur* –

The more I read and experience,
the more I find humans to
be complicated creatures.
We have great flaws
but also great strengths.
I love this portrayal of Lancelot
because it captures
the contradictions of the human
condition so well.

66

They say, that the Princess, having made due reflection on
the perseverance of her lover, his discretion, and all the
good qualities of his mind, his wit and judgment, saw no
longer the deformity of his body, nor the ugliness of his
face; that his hump seemed to her no more than the homely
air of one who has a broad back; and that whereas till then
she saw him limp horribly, she found it nothing more than a
certain sidling air, which charmed her.

99

– Charles Perrault, *The Fairy Tales of Charles Perrault*,
"Riquet with the Tuft" –

I must say,
this quotation feels
particularly apt.

"

Honour and virtue are the ornaments of the mind, without which the body, though it be so, has no right to pass for beautiful.

"

– Miguel de Cervantes, *Don Quixote* –

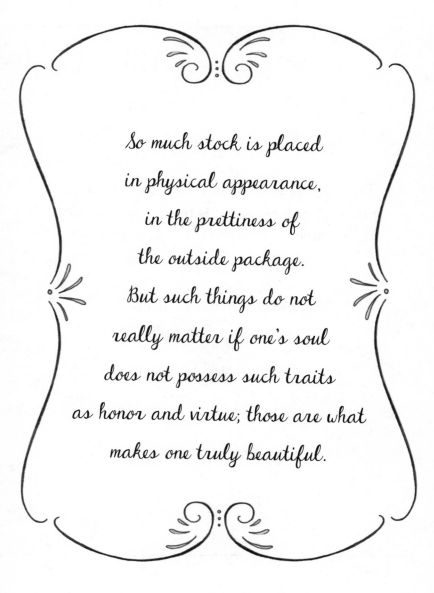

So much stock is placed
in physical appearance,
in the prettiness of
the outside package.
But such things do not
really matter if one's soul
does not possess such traits
as honor and virtue; those are what
makes one truly beautiful.

"

The tiny Lilliputians surmise that Gulliver's watch
may be his god, because it is that which, he admits,
he seldom does anything without consulting.

"

– Jonathan Swift, *Gulliver's Travels* –

I think Cogsworth
might appreciate
Monsieur Swift's
observation here.

"

We'll let time knit these gentle ties between us.

"

– Molière, *The Misanthrope* –

Time is indeed quite
mighty. It can
heal
wounds
and build
friendships when
one least expects it.

"

There are persons to whom one does not dare to give any other marks of the love one feels for them than those which do not affect them in any but an indirect way; and since one does not dare to show one's love, one would at least desire that they should see that one wishes not to be loved by any one else. One would like to have them know that there is no beauty, of whatever rank, whom one would not regard with indifference, and that there is no crown which one would wish to buy at the price of never seeing them.

"

– Madame de La Fayette, *The Princess of Clèves* –

This feels like such
a real observation.
It can be difficult to express
love—particularly the very
beginnings of love, the first few
chapters. But that does not
diminish its sincerity.

"

The course of true love never did run smooth.

""

– William Shakespeare, *A Midsummer Night's Dream* –

I like to imagine love as a curving
         river—one that at times must carve
new streams through parched lands
      and push through rocky paths, and at other
      times rushes and flows with greater ease.
            Its path is full of
                  twists and turns—and
                        surprises.

"

'Paráventure it may the better be:
These oldë folk know muchë thing,' quoth she.

"

– Geoffrey Chaucer, *The Canterbury Tales*, "The Wife of Bath's Tale" –

Our elders are often ignored,
but they have great
stories to tell, if you
are listening.
With age often comes
great wisdom.

"

My salad days,
When I was green in judgment, cold in blood,
To say as I said then!

"

– William Shakespeare, *Antony and Cleopatra* –

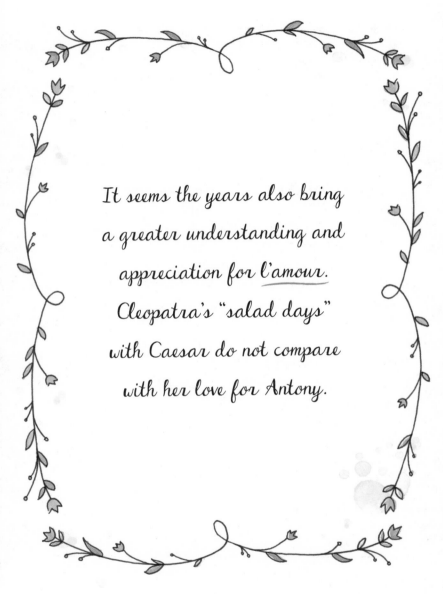

It seems the years also bring
a greater understanding and
appreciation for *l'amour.*
Cleopatra's "salad days"
with Caesar do not compare
with her love for Antony.

"

A judge, replied the Empress, is easy to be had, but to get an impartial judge, is a thing so difficult.

"

– Margaret Cavendish, *The Blazing World* –

Madame Cavendish
is quite right.
We all bring our own biases
and past experiences to each
situation. It can be quite
<u>difficile</u>
to be completely objective.

"

He fancied himself to have reached a famous castle
(for, as has been said, all the inns he lodged in were
castles to his eyes).

"

– Miguel de Cervantes, *Don Quixote* –

Quixote, par exemple, has a unique
take on every situation he encounters.
A castle or an inn—you see,
it all depends on one's
perspective.

"

Ambition and gallantry were the sole occupation of the court, busying men and women alike.

"

– Madame de La Fayette, *The Princess of Clèves* –

I have often read of the ferocious
nature of the courts—of the lords
and ladies focusing solely
on their strategies
to obtain power.
Should not such an elevated
position be used to help those
less fortunate?

66

And men should be quite other than they are.
But is their lack of righteousness a reason
To shun the world? These faults of human nature
But give us opportunities in life
To put in practice our philosophy;
This is the best employment virtue finds.

99

– Molière, *The Misanthrope* –

For all of mankind's faults,
we cannot give up on the human race.
I know firsthand that there is good
in this world, that people can change.
And therefore, there is hope.

"

My reason tells me so
Each day. But reason does not govern love.

"

– Molière, *The Misanthrope* –

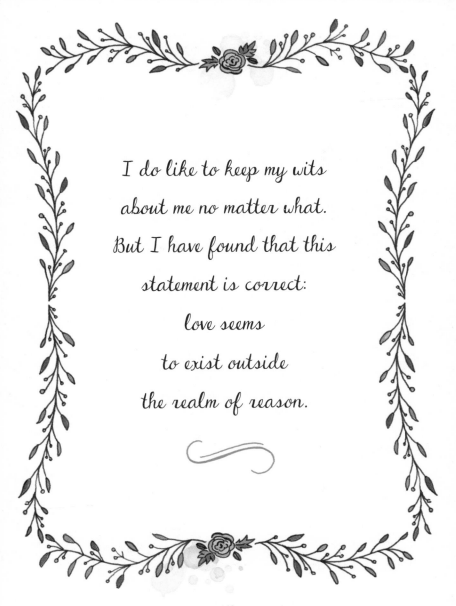

I do like to keep my wits
about me no matter what.
But I have found that this
statement is correct:
love seems
to exist outside
the realm of reason.

"

Love can transpose to form and dignity.
Love looks not with the eyes, but with the mind,
And therefore is winged Cupid painted blind.

"

– William Shakespeare, *A Midsummer Night's Dream* –

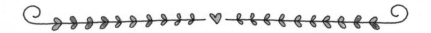

Love can be beautiful, strange, powerful.
It can be blind
to what the rest of the world sees,
perceiving something else entirely.
It can even be transformative.

"

Now you know that it is possible for even a Mouse to confer benefits on a Lion.

"

– Aesop, *Aesop's Fables*, "The Lion and the Mouse" –

This passage reminds me
of little Chip.
Though he be small, he can
do great things.

"

Undoubtedly philosophers are in the right, when they tell us that nothing is great or little otherwise than by comparison.

"

– Jonathan Swift, *Gulliver's Travels* –

Another excellent point!
Grand or petit—
size is merely
a matter of perspective.

"

Imagine with thyself, courteous reader, how often I then wished for the tongue of Demosthenes or Cicero, that might have enabled me to celebrate the praise of my own dear native country, in a style equal to its merits and felicity.

"

– Jonathan Swift, *Gulliver's Travels* –

Oh, how I relate to Monsieur Swift's
woes here. I have often wished
I could come up with a description
as lyrical as Milton's, an observation
as profound as Plato's.
There are so many great
masters of language.
They are magically eloquent,
and I aspire to be like them.

"

In short, he became so absorbed in his books that he spent
his nights from sunset to sunrise, and his days from dawn
to dark, poring over them; and what with little sleep and
much reading his brains got so dry that he lost his wits.
His fancy grew full of what he used to read about in
his books, enchantments, quarrels, battles, challenges,
wounds, wooings, loves, agonies, and all sorts of impossible
nonsense; and it so possessed his mind that the whole
fabric of invention and fancy he read of was true, that to
him no history in the world had more reality in it.

"

– Miguel de Cervantes, *Don Quixote* –

Quixote's tale is so fascinating to me.
To be that caught up in
one's reading, to have
books come to life
so vividly and overwhelmingly.
It seems at once a blessing and a
curse to live in a haze of fiction.

"

Having tasted the honeycomb, he threw down his axe, and looking on the tree as sacred, took great care of it.

"

– Aesop, *Aesop's Fables*, "The Peasant and the Apple-Tree" –

Nature provides so many extraordinary
bits of nourishment and splendor for us.
I certainly feel we should return the
favor in any small way we can.

"

Sweet moon, I thank thee for thy sunny beams.
I thank thee, moon, for shining now so bright.

"

– William Shakespeare, *A Midsummer Night's Dream* –

Is there anything so
beautiful
as the faithful,
ever-illuminating
moon?

"

For nature is so full of variety, that our weak senses cannot
perceive all the various sorts of her creatures.

"

– Margaret Cavendish, *The Blazing World* –

How I love to wander through the castle
gardens. Just as no two branches on
a single tree are alike, nor two petals on
a single rose, there is immense variety
in everything nature creates.
And in such diversity
lies beauty.

"

And so I go through these solitudes and wilds seeking
adventures, resolved in soul to oppose my arm and person
to the most perilous that fortune may offer me in aid of the
weak and needy.

"

– Miguel de Cervantes, *Don Quixote* –

I love this image
of Quixote embarking
on his quest of
knighthood
and
chivalry!

"

[I] yearned to go with them and enjoy the sight of strange countries, and I longed for the society of the various races of mankind and for traffic and profit.

"

– Anonymous, *The Book of the Thousand Nights and a Night*,
"The Fourth Voyage of Sindbad the Seaman" –

Indeed, there is nothing more
rewarding than seeking
adventure, exploring the wide world
in all its variety,
its messiness, its loveliness.

"

'I have heard say,' said Don Quixote,
'that he who sings scares away his woes.'

"

– Miguel de Cervantes, *Don Quixote* –

This quotation reminds me
of Maestro Cadenza.
He understands more than
most the power of music.

"

And after that the melody heard he,
That cometh of those spherës thricë three,
That wells of music be and melody
In this world here, and cause of harmony.

"

– Geoffrey Chaucer, "The Assembly of Fowls" –

Indeed,
a single song,
a single dance can
express emotions
like nothing else,
and can connect
and bring souls together
in a harmony that
is profound
and moving.

"

Since Fortune and the Fates would give me none, I have made a world of my own: for which no body, I hope, will blame me, since it is in every one's power to do the like.

"

– Margaret Cavendish, *The Blazing World* –

What a pleasing idea—
if you are not satisfied
with the world or your
current circumstances
within it, you have the power
to create your own!

“

Then I defy you, stars!

”

– William Shakespeare, *Romeo and Juliet* –

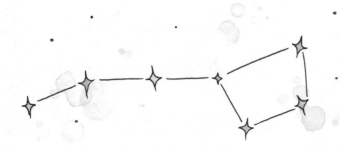

I have found much about fate
in my reading. It is true: sometimes
we are simply given a bad lot—a bad
example to follow, perhaps.
But why not try to make our
destinies, to build our own
constellations (to borrow Monsieur
Shakespeare's metaphor)?
I have often wanted so much more
than what I thought the world
had planned for me.

"

I wish you both every day to look into the mirror: you,
my son, that you may not spoil your beauty by evil conduct;
and you, my daughter, that you may make up for your want
of beauty by your virtues.

"

– Aesop, *Aesop's Fables*, "The Brother and the Sister" –

Mirrors can be
tricky things.
Sometimes they display
the truth, sometimes only
a piece of it. They should
be used with the utmost care.

"

For it will happen that when one thing
is looked for another thing is found.

"

– Miguel de Cervantes, *Don Quixote* –

I love Monsieur
Cervantes's line here.
Perhaps we do not often
seek out what will be
best for us, but end up,
eventually, finding it
standing before us anyway.

66

For madam, said Sir Launcelot, I love not to be constrained to love; for love must arise of the heart, and not by no constraint. That is truth, said the king, and many knight's love is free in himself, and never will be bounden, for where he is bounden he looseth himself.

99

– Sir Thomas Malory, *Le Morte d'Arthur* –

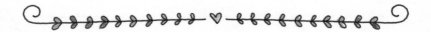

L'amour—what a complicated thing.
It cannot be forced or tamed,
and often it comes when
one least expects it.

"

My bounty is as boundless as the sea,
My love as deep. The more I give to thee
The more I have, for both are infinite.

"

– William Shakespeare, *Romeo and Juliet* –

A beautiful sentiment.
True love is selfless;
it does not ask for too much,
does not drain or take away.
True love is abundant.

"

They may create worlds of their own, and govern
themselves as they please: but yet let them have a care,
not to prove unjust usurpers, and to rob me of mine;
for concerning the Philosophical World, I am Empress
of it myself.

"

– Margaret Cavendish, *The Blazing World* –

Madame Cavendish's point reminds me that books are entire worlds unto themselves, transporting us (sometimes quite literally, in my experience) to new places. There is great power for authors and readers both in such creation and exploration.

❝

For there is no book so bad
but it has something good in it.

❞

– Miguel de Cervantes, *Don Quixote* –

I couldn't agree more!

Appendix

FOR MORE DETAILS ABOUT THE TITLES QUOTED
IN *BELLE'S LIBRARY* AND WHY THEY WERE
CHOSEN, READ ON. THE EDITIONS FOR
THE WORKS THAT HAVE BEEN TRANSLATED
OR MODERNIZED FROM THE ORIGINAL
ARE ALSO NOTED.

AESOP'S FABLES
by Aesop

Believed to have been created
in the late to mid-sixth century BCE

EDITION USED:
George Routledge and Sons
London, 1867
Translated by George Fyler Townsend
Illustrations designed by Harrison Weir
and engraved by J. Greenaway

This collection of fables is one of the oldest examples of storytelling around. It is credited to Aesop, a slave in ancient Greece, and was originally shared orally. The short tales each contain some sort of moral and often feature animals with human characteristics. Since they were first created, the fables have been translated and published numerous times in countries all over the world, with various editions and iterations. Many of the stories still resonate today, such as the famous race between the Tortoise and the Hare.

As one of the most famous texts in Western literature, Aesop's work would have been familiar to Belle. Having a strong moral compass herself, she most certainly would have appreciated the themes and lessons from the various tales, such as the importance of inner beauty and hard work.

Pages where quotations appear: 30, 46, 60, 78, 82, 100, 146, 154, 172

ANTONY AND CLEOPATRA
by William Shakespeare

Originally published in 1623 as *The Tragedy of Antony and Cleopatra*

Based on Plutarch's series of Greek and Roman biographies, *Lives*, this play follows Cleopatra and Mark Antony's historically complicated relationship. It opens about two years after the events of Shakespeare's earlier work, *Julius Caesar*, and takes place over a ten-year span during a tumultuous period in the Roman Empire.

Filled with drama, passion, and heartbreak, this play would have fascinated Belle with its numerous examples of how power and leadership can go wrong. She would also have appreciated the themes of love's many complexities and the power of the steady march of time, which can drastically change things.

Pages where quotations appear: 114, 132

THE BLAZING WORLD
by Margaret Cavendish

Originally published in 1666 as *The Description of a New World, Called the Blazing-World*

Margaret Cavendish's book is considered one of the earliest forerunners of science fiction. In it, a young woman travels to a utopian world filled with different species of talking animals who are very civil and kind. She soon becomes empress of the land, asking many questions about life there and how it can be improved. She enacts various laws regarding the society and scientific advancements of the world and learns more about numerous worlds in the universe.

Filled with philosophy and adventure, *The Blazing World* is a unique, creative title. Belle would have enjoyed the themes of travel, discovery, and friendship, and would have found the many questions it poses thought-provoking. She would also have appreciated Cavendish's belief that everyone has the power to create his or her own world.

Pages where quotations appear: 48, 88, 92, 134, 158, 168, 180

THE BOOK OF THE
THOUSAND NIGHTS
AND A NIGHT
by Anonymous

Believed to have been created before
the tenth century CE

EDITION USED:
The Burton Club
London, 1885
Translated by Sir Richard Francis Burton

Also referred to as *One Thousand and One Nights* and *The Arabian Nights*, this collection is largely made up of Middle Eastern and South Asian stories and folktales. The origin of the collection is still a bit of a mystery, but its earliest mention is in a Persian text from the tenth century.

The tales all fall within one main frame story, which follows Shahrázád, the clever daughter of a vizier, who saves herself from execution by a tyrant king by telling him a captivating story every evening. She always ends on a cliffhanger with a promise to finish it the next night, delaying her execution repeatedly until the king abandons his cruel plan.

Belle would not only have enjoyed the heroine's cunning plan to save the day with the power of storytelling, she would also have appreciated all the imaginative and compelling tales set in another part of the world.

Pages where quotations appear: 40, 52, 58, 106, 162

THE CANTERBURY TALES
by Geoffrey Chaucer

Originally published in 1478

EDITION USED:
W. W. Swayne
Brooklyn, 1870
Edited by David Laing Purves

The Canterbury Tales was originally written in Middle English and is considered an important work in Western literature. Similar to *The Book of the Thousand Nights and a Night*, this book features a frame story for its numerous tales: a group of individuals of different stations and professions makes a long pilgrimage from London to Canterbury and decides to hold a storytelling contest in order to pass the time. The book is made up of their tales, which cover everything from fate to love to society to religion. This edition includes Chaucer's poem "The Assembly of Fowls," which is also quoted in this book.

Belle would most likely have been very familiar with the famous *Canterbury Tales* during her time period. The variety among the stories in writing style, tone, and subject matter would have been quite appealing. It would have been almost like having twenty-four books in one!

Pages where quotations appear: 38, 64, 72, 76, 104, 108, 130, 166

DON QUIXOTE
by Miguel de Cervantes

Originally published in 1605 (Part I)
and 1615 (Part II) as *The Ingenious Gentleman
Don Quixote of La Mancha*

EDITION USED:
Macmillan
New York, 1885
Translated by John Ormsby

Miguel de Cervantes's work follows a Spanish nobleman who becomes so engrossed in all the books he reads about knights, honor, and romance that he decides to become a knight and bring back the age of chivalry. He recruits a farmer named Sancho to accompany him as his squire. The plot follows their quests and friendship, with Quixote often believing he is in a harrowing knight's tale instead of the real world and Sancho doing his best to help him.

Don Quixote was very well received when it was first published and is still considered one of the greatest and most influential works in Western literature. The story would have been right up Belle's alley with its examples of adventure, its nostalgia for a time of knights and chivalry, and its demonstration of the power of reading.

Pages where quotations appear: 50, 56, 68, 70, 94, 120, 136, 152, 160, 164, 174, 182

THE FAIRY TALES OF CHARLES PERRAULT
by Charles Perrault

Originally published in 1697

EDITION USED:
George G. Harrap & Co. Ltd.
London, 1922
Translated by Robert Samber

In 1697, French author Charles Perrault published this collection of fairy tales based on stories that had been passed down orally for generations upon generations. Many of the fairy tales in Perrault's book are still well-known today, such as his takes on Little Red Riding Hood, Sleeping Beauty, and Cinderella. There are also more obscure tales in this collection, from a story about a fairy enchanting a kind girl so that jewels fall out of her mouth when she speaks, to an account of a woodcutter being rash with wishes. Each tale ends with some sort of moral or key takeaway.

As they were published and quite popular in her native France, Belle would probably have grown up with these fairy tales igniting her imagination and sparking her love of reading. In fact, some of the magical elements in these tales might have come to mind as she encountered the enchanted castle.

Pages where quotations appear: 24, 34, 66, 80, 96, 110, 112, 118

GULLIVER'S TRAVELS
by Jonathan Swift

Originally published in 1726

Gulliver's Travels was quite popular and controversial when it was first published. Jonathan Swift wrote the book, a satire on society and human nature, during a very politically charged time in Ireland and England. The book follows Lemuel Gulliver on his adventures to many foreign lands, including Lilliput, an island populated by tiny people; Brobdingnag, a kingdom of giants; and the land of the Houyhnhnms, a race of philosophical talking horses.

Belle would have appreciated Swift's critique of society. Perhaps it would have reminded her of the problems and prejudices she saw in her small village. In addition, with her strong desire for adventure, she would have enjoyed Gulliver's journeys to various lands filled with interesting characters.

Pages where quotations appear: 42, 54, 122, 148, 150

A MIDSUMMER
NIGHT'S DREAM
by William Shakespeare

Originally published in 1600

A *Midsummer Night's Dream* is one of Shakespeare's most famous comedies. The play features whimsical and fantastic elements such as fairies, love potions, and references to Greek mythology. It takes place in an enchanted forest and follows a duke and queen about to get married, a quarreling fairy king and queen, a group of amateur actors, and four young lovers who are subjected to various antics by the mischievous fairies.

Belle expresses her love of Shakespeare in the film and also quotes this play. She would surely have enjoyed the work's imaginative qualities as well as its commentary on the complications of love.

Pages where quotations appear: 102, 128, 144, 156

THE MISANTHROPE
by Molière

Originally published in 1666

EDITION USED:
G. P. Putnam's Sons
New York, 1908
Translated by Curtis Hidden Page

Molière's comedy of manners examines and pokes fun at French aristocracy. It follows a misanthrope named Alceste who, refusing to follow the conventions of society, is always brutally honest. While filled with humor, this play also features complex and multidimensional characters, differentiating it from other satires, which often focus on stereotypes.

It seems likely that Belle would have enjoyed this work by a popular French playwright with its clever and amusing insights into society, love, and human nature. She would also have appreciated the multifaceted characters thanks to her great understanding that people have many layers underneath the first impressions they make.

Pages where quotations appear: 28, 44, 90, 124, 140, 142

LE MORTE D'ARTHUR
by Sir Thomas Malory

Originally published in 1485

EDITION USED:
J. M. Dent & Sons Ltd.
London, 1906

Tales about the legendary King Arthur and the knights of the Round Table have been around for centuries, but Malory's epic work is among the best known and serves as the principal source for study and inspiration. Writing in Middle English, Malory was influenced by both French and English sources. His book follows King Arthur's mythic life and the many characters that affect it, such as Lancelot and Guinevere.

This is a work that both Belle and the Beast reference in the film. It transports readers into the world of knights and chivalry and explores the complications of honor, love, and leadership. Perhaps most profoundly, it examines what it means to be a good king, a good knight, and a good man. These are things the Beast struggles with as well, and Belle would have found such themes quite poignant and absorbing.

Pages where quotations appear: 84, 116, 176

THE ODYSSEY
by Homer

Believed to have been created
in the late eighth century BCE

EDITION USED:
William Heinemann
London, 1919
Translated by A. T. Murray

The *Odyssey* is another classic that was originally shared in the oral tradition. This epic is attributed to Homer, a blind poet who probably lived during the eighth century BCE. A follow-up to the *Iliad*, the *Odyssey* follows the Greek hero Odysseus on his perilous journey home from the Trojan War. Meanwhile, his wife, Penelope, and son, Telemachus, must protect their home from a band of rowdy and aggressive suitors seeking to take Odysseus's place.

Texts originating in ancient Greece have been translated, studied, and enjoyed for centuries, and Belle would most likely have had a version of Homer's works in her library. She would have enjoyed Penelope's resourcefulness and the grand episodes that make up Odysseus's adventures. The references to the importance of hospitality might have reminded her of the warm welcome from Lumiere and the rest of the friendly staff.

Pages where quotations appear: 32, 74

OROONOKO
by Aphra Behn

Originally published in 1688 as *Oroonoko: or, the Royal Slave*

Author Aphra Behn's life story is a fascinating one. At one time a spy for Charles II, Behn was one of the first English women to earn her living by writing. *Oroonoko* is a controversial novel about an African prince who is unjustly taken into slavery. Though it is a complicated text with some contradicting views that are pointed out today, it in many ways presents an anticolonial view that was radical during its time period.

Belle would have been moved by some of the themes of the book, such as the problems with "othering," or seeing groups of people as inherently different and alien, and therefore inferior. Belle witnesses this phenomenon in her own life, such as when the villagers attack the Beast and his castle because they fear his beastly appearance.

Pages where quotations appear: 22, 86

THE PRINCESS OF CLÈVES
by Madame de La Fayette

Originally published in 1678

EDITION USED:
Little, Brown, and Company
Boston, 1891
Translated by Thomas Sergeant Perry
Illustrations drawn by Jules Garnier
and engraved by A. Lamotte

The Princess of Clèves was originally published anonymously but is believed to have been written by Madame de La Fayette. It follows a young woman in the French court who is torn between duty and love. Largely considered the first psychological novel, this book has influenced many famous works after it. Though its heroine is fictional, it is also filled with historical figures and events and is said to be a realistic portrayal of Henry II's royal French court.

The Princess of Clèves was quite popular when it was originally published in Paris, and it sparked controversy over its anonymous authorship, subject matter, and ambiguous ending. Belle would have most certainly wanted to read such an intriguing and buzzed-about French title. She would also have been enthralled by its realism, philosophies, and themes regarding the complexity of people and of love.

Pages where quotations appear: 36, 98, 126, 138

ROMEO AND JULIET
by William Shakespeare

Originally published in 1599 as The Most Excellent and Lamentable Tragedy of Romeo and Juliet

This tragedy was one of Shakespeare's most popular works during his time period, and it remains one of his most popular works today. Inspired by an Italian tale and an English poem, it follows two star-crossed young lovers who want more than anything to be together despite the fact that their families are enemies.

Belle mentions that *Romeo and Juliet* is her favorite play in the film. She would have loved the beautiful poetic language, the romance of a love story with considerable obstacles, and the commentary on society and convention. Of course, she and the Beast are also an unlikely pair who face many a hurdle in their own story.

Pages where quotations appear: 20, 170, 178

THE ROVER
by Aphra Behn

Originally published in 1677 as *The Rover: or, the Banish't Cavaliers*

When Charles II refused to pay Aphra Behn for her services as a spy, she turned to writing and became one of the first English women to earn her living as an author. Her play *The Rover* follows a group of English Cavaliers and their escapades at a carnival in Naples. It weaves together multiple plotlines featuring a variety of characters, including a trio of Spanish siblings who have complications in their love lives.

Inspired by another play, *Thomaso*, this Restoration comedy further develops the female characters, making them complex, distinct, and full of agency. Belle would have enjoyed *The Rover*'s examination and critique of class distinctions and gender roles as well as its strong female characters. She would have found Behn's own history fascinating and empowering.

Pages where quotations appear: 26, 62